Ohh Ohhh I knew That.......

Stories of Old Man Joe

By Miss Lisa Pizza
Aka Lisa Maria McGlone

Pictures by Mercedes Jordan

LifeRich Publishing is a registered trademark of The Reader's Digest Association, Inc.

LifeRich Publishing books may be ordered through booksellers or by contacting:

LifeRich Publishing
1663 Liberty Drive
Bloomington, IN 47403
www.liferichpublishing.com
1 (888) 238-8637

Because of the dynamic nature of the Internet, any web addresses or links contained
in this book may have changed since publication and may no longer be valid. The views
expressed in this work are solely those of the author and do not necessarily reflect the views
of the publisher, and the publisher hereby disclaims any responsibility for them.

Any people depicted in stock imagery provided by Thinkstock are models,
and such images are being used for illustrative purposes only.
Certain stock imagery © Thinkstock.

ISBN: 978-1-4897-0806-9 (sc)
ISBN: 978-1-4897-0807-6 (hc)
ISBN: 978-1-4897-0805-2 (e)

Print information available on the last page.

LifeRich Publishing rev. date: 05/06/2016

This book is dedicated to Evora Mae Holliday and
Evora "Cherice" McGlone! My lovely mother and my
beautiful daughter. I love you both! Lisa

"To both of my grandmothers, who I've only
ever met in my dreams" Mercedes

Contents

Hello, Friends! My name is Lisa M. McGlone. But, you can call me Miss Lisa Pizza! I'd like to introduce you to OLD MAN JOE! He is a funny character that I created more than 20 years ago! Old Man Joe is simply a silly man, who was the result of a good imagination. He has everyday adventures that most of us have experienced or will experience throughout our lifetime. Old Man Joe turns an ordinary experience into a hilarious adventure. Elementary school children all over the world will enjoy and connect to Old Man Joe through his hilarious adventures and his famous saying, "Oh Ohh I Knew That!"

Story One

Old Man Joe Goes To an Elementary School

Old Man Joe Goes to Elementary School

Old Man Joe was a silly old man. The silliest old man you ever did see. Well, it seems, one day, Old Man Joe was walking down the street when he saw a sign that said 'School'.

"Oh Oh" said Old Man Joe. "I want to go to school. I want to go to school!" so, Old Man Joe walked into the building. As he entered the building, there was a lady behind a desk. "Excuuse me," said Old Man Joe. "I want to go to school! I want to go to school!" "Well," said the security guard. "First, I need an i.d" Old Man Joe got a baffled look on his face and said, "Why do you need my eye??? And my name is Old Man Joe not D!!!!"

The security guard laughed and laughed and said, "Old Man Joe you are a silly old man. An i.d. means an identification telling us who you are" Old Man Joe thought about it and said, *__"Oh..Oh I knew that. Oh Oh..... I knew that!"__*

The Security Assistant gave Old Man Joe a visitor's badge, and off he went towards the cafeteria.

When he got to the cafeteria Old Man Joe said, "Excuuuuuse me Excuuuse me I want to get some lunch!" The cafeteria manager looked up from serving and said in a stern voice, "Sir you need to wait in line before you can get some food!" Disappointed Old Man Joe dropped his head and slowly walked over to the monitor and said, " Excuuuuuse me. Excuuuuuse me can you tell me where the line is? Without even looking up, the monitor said, " the teacher's lounge is across the hall on the......Old Man Joe scratched his head and said "That's where I get my lunch??" "Ohhhh" the lady said. "The line to get lunch is right there behind those children." Old Man Joe got a sheepish look and said***"Oh..Oh I knew that. Oh Oh..... I knew that!"***

When he got to the serving line, Old Man Joe said, "I'll have a double cheeseburger, a chilidog, fries, an apple pie and a sweet tea. And don't you try to fool me, I saw the commercial and that's part of the $5.00 bag."

The server laughed till she turned red. In between laughs, she said, "Old Man Joe you are a silly old man! This is not a fast food restaurant. This a school cafeteria. You may have a fish sandwich, mashed potatoes, an apple, and a chocolate milk." Old Man Joe took his cafeteria tray and said, ***"Oh..Oh I knew that. Oh Oh..... I knew that!"*** Old Man Joe sat at a table and began having a conversation.

He asked a little boy, "What will you do next?" When the boy said he was going to p.e., of course Old Man Joe got confused. He became hysterical laughing loudly and spewing food. When the monitor rushed over to see what was going on, Old Man Joe kept saying, "He has to go pee-pee" The monitor explained that P.E means physical education. And Old Man Joe said ***"Oh..Oh I knew that. Oh Oh..... I knew that!"***

Old Man Joe caused such a disruption that the Security Lady asked him to leave and never come back.

And that is the story of Old Man Joe goes to an elementary school.

Story 2:

Old Man Joe Goes to Church

Old Man Joe Goes to Church

Old Man Joe was a silly old man! The silliest old man ever did see. Well it seems that one day old man Joe was walking down a road when he saw a church. Outside of the church was a sign that read, 'Please come in. All are welcome'

Old Man Joe said, "ooooh I want to go to church!" So Old Man Joe entered the beautiful building and stared in awe at the amazing stained glass windows for a few moments. When the greeter approached, Old Man Joe said, "Excuse me. Excuse me. I want to go church!" "Very well," said the greeter. "Why don't you have a seat on the pew."

Old Man Joe proceeded to the church bench and pulled a small can of air freshener from his pocket and began spraying uncontrollably.

Everyone started coughing and gasping. The usher walked over and said in his best British voice, ""Pardon me, Sir. WHAT are you doing???? "Old Man Joe stopped spraying, and answered, " I was trying to make the seats smell good. The man told me to sit on a pew!" The usher and all of the people in the area laughed and laughed. The usher replied, "Old Man Joe you are a silly old man! A pew is the name of a church bench----not the smell of a church bench." Old Man Joe was so embarrassed. ***Oh! Oh......*** ***I knew that! Oh Oh..... I knew that!!!!!"*** He said.

Old Man Joe took a seat and began to enjoy the church service. After a few powerful songs, the Pastor of the church stood up smiling and sweating. "didn't this choir sinnnnnng??" he said in his deep baritone voice. He continued, "And I don't know about you, but I love their new robes! Church aren't these robes gorgeous?!" Old Man Joe was puzzled. He stood up and raised his hand.

"Excuuuuse me. " He said. "Where did they come from? Kmart or Target? The Pastor and the congregation looked at him. Finally, the Pastor spoke. "I am not sure what you are talking about Son. " Old Man Joe continued talking. "The Pastor said they had on new robes and I was just wondering, did the new robes come from Kmart or Target because I always buy my robes from Wal-Mart and I ain't never seen no robes like that." The entire church erupted in laughter!

"Old Man Joe you are a silly old man!" They all said. The Pastor continued. "The choir robes are specially ordered for the people who are up here singing. This is their uniform!" Old Man Joe looked around and sunk down into his pew. ***<u>"Oh. Oh...... I Knew that. Oh Ohh I knew that!!!"</u>*** he mumbled.

Towards the end of church, the Pastor announced, "It is time for us to collect the offering. This morning we would like to raise a special offering for our homeless friends who have no shelter. Baskets traveled up one aisle and down the next.

When the basket finished traveling down Old Man Joe's aisle, the usher realized that the basket was empty. Quickly, the usher rushed to the pulpit to speak to the Pastor. The Pastor walked to the microphone and cleared his voice. "Brothers and Sisters we seem to have a problem. Someone has stolen our church offering!"One of the members pointed to Old Man Joe and shouted, "He did it! He did it!" Old Man Joe stood and spoke.

"Your honor, I haven't stolen anything. I thought this was my money. I heard you say, the offering was for our friends with no shelter. I just called the park the other day and they said that there were no shelters to rent for my cookout, sooooooo I don't have a shelter." Once again, the entire church erupted in chuckles. The Pastor caught breath and said, "Old Man Joe you are a silly old man! This offering is for people who don't have any place to call home. A shelter over their heads."

Old Man Joe felt his heart drop and his face turned red! "Oh Oh I knew that!!!! Oh Oh I knew that!!"

Old Man Joe headed toward the exit.

It wasn't going to take a rocket scientist to tell him his church visit was over.

Story three

Old Man Joe Goes to the Baseball Game

Old Man Joe goes to a Baseball Game

Old Man Joe was a silly old man. The silliest old man you ever did see. Well it seems one day, Old Man Joe was walking down the street and he saw a sign advertising a baseball game.

"Ohhh Ohhh!" said Old Man Joe to himself. I want to go to a baseball game. So Old Man purchased a ticket and entered the stadium. Old Man Joe walked up to the usher and said, " to see a baseball game." "Great!" replied the usher. "Go have a seat on the bleachers."

Old Man Joe got a bit agitated and said, "Hey, I didn't come to wash my clothes I don't need any bleach!!!" The usher got very tickled. "Old Man Joe you are a silly old man. Bleachers are the seats you sit in at a stadium." Old Man Joe gave the usher a sheepish grin. "Ohh Ohh I knew that! Ohh Ohhh I knew that" he said. So Old Man Joe was seated beside a family with a very excited 9 year old little boy. The little boy said, "Hey Mister! Do you wanna see my new mitt?" Old Man Joe looked down at him.

"Sure, where do you live?" he asked. The boy panicked and started yelling, "STRANGER DANGER!" The boys' father stood up. "Hey guy. What's the big idea??" Old Man Joe was confused. "Sir the little boy asked me if I want to see his new mitt and I wanted to see it and see if it matched the dish towels and other stuff in the kitchen." By this time, the usher who had seated him had come back. When he heard the story, he laughed again. "Old Man Joe you are a silly old man. A mitt is another name for a glove! Before you ask not winter gloves, a baseball glove." Old Man Joe looked at the angry people. "Ohh Ohh I knew that! Ohh Ohhh I knew that!"

The usher showed him to another seat. Old Man Joe was enjoying the game until he heard the crowd yelling, "slide! Slide!" Of course Old Man Joe did not know what they meant, so he stood up and began to do the dance called 'the electric slide'.

The usher came down to see what all the commotion was about. Old Man Joe explained about the dance and why he was dancing to the electric slide. This time the usher laughed till he cried. "Old Man Joe you are a silly old man!" he said. "Slide means for the player to run and fall toward the base to avoid being tagged by the other team" Old Man Joe smiled an embarrassed smile and said, "Ohhh Ohhh I knew that! Ohh I knew that!" Once again, the kind usher was about to show Old Man Joe to another seat, when the crowd yelled,

"He's OUT!" Naturally, Old Man Joe thought they were referring to him. Sadly he turned towards the exit.

The usher did not even bother to tell him of his error. Instead he waved goodbye and returned to his job hoping not to see Old Man Joe again.

Old Man Joe Goes to the Pool

Old Man Joe Goes to the Pool

Old Man Joe was a silly old man. The silliest old man you ever did see. Well it seems one day, Old Man Joe was walking down the street and he saw a sign that said, 'Swimming pool open today at noon.'

"Ohhh" said Old Man Joe. "I want to go the pool" so Old Man Joe went into the gate and spoke to the lifeguard. "Excuuuuse me. My name is Old Man Joe and I want to use the swimming pool." He said in a very excited voice. The lifeguard looked at Old Man Joe and smiled.

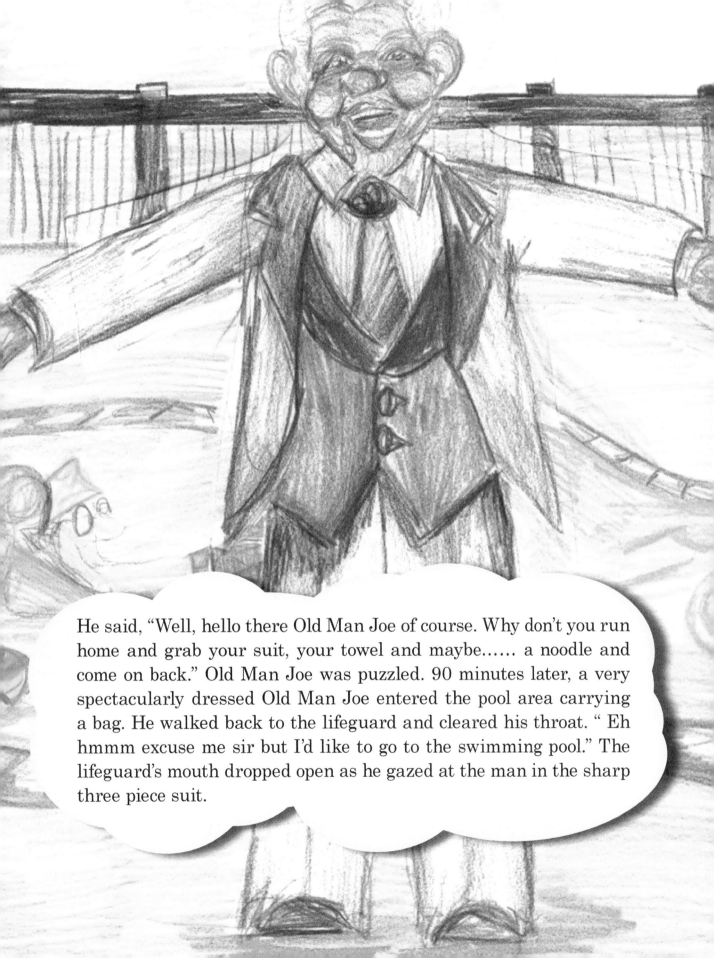

He said, "Well, hello there Old Man Joe of course. Why don't you run home and grab your suit, your towel and maybe…… a noodle and come on back." Old Man Joe was puzzled. 90 minutes later, a very spectacularly dressed Old Man Joe entered the pool area carrying a bag. He walked back to the lifeguard and cleared his throat. " Eh hmmm excuse me sir but I'd like to go to the swimming pool." The lifeguard's mouth dropped open as he gazed at the man in the sharp three piece suit.

"May I help you?" the lifeguard asked. Old Man Joe cleared his throat and said in a rather irritated voice, "I am Old Man Joe!" you told me to go home and get my suit!" the lifeguard scratched his head and said, "Old Man Joe you are a silly old man. You have to have on a swimming suit if you want to go swimming. That suit is for going to work" Old Man Joe looked at himself and the others in the pool. "Ohh Ohhh I Knew that! Ohhhh Oh I knew that!" He mumbled. The lifeguard looked at the bag that Old Man Joe was carrying. Old Man Joe grinned and said," Oh yeah, I bought the towel. As a matter of fact, I brought enough towels to share."

Old Man Joe reached into his bag and pulled out a roll of paper towels. The lifeguard thought he would explode with laughter. "Old Man Joe you are a silly old man" he said between laughs. "When I said bring a towel, I meant a big, beach towel, not lots of paper towels. You can't dry yourself off with a paper towel." Old Man Joe felt so embarrassed. " Ohhh Ohhh I knew that! Ohhhh. Ohhh I knew that" Old Man Joe looked in his bag. "Why don't you take this? I probably won't be needing it at the pool today." said Old Man Joe. He handed the lifeguard an uncooked package of Ramen Noodles.

The lifeguard shook his head in disbelief. "Old MAN Joe you are a silly old man!" he said as Old Man Joe walked away.

About the Author

Lisa M. McGlone is an elementary school teacher, published poet, (It's All About You......A Book of Poems written especially for special People Like You firstbooks-2004) licensed minister, storyteller, and, an avid Redskin fan! She grew up in Silver Spring Md. Lisa graduated from North Carolina Central University. She is currently completing her 31st year as a public school teacher in the Virginia Beach (Va.) Public Schools. When Lisa is working in her church (New Life Church-Pastor Dan Backens) 4 and 5 year old class, she is affectionately known as Miss Lisa Pizza! Lisa has one beautiful, amazing daughter, Evora Cherice, who graduated from Howard University in 2014 and currently works in corporate America.

About the Illustrator

Mercedes Jordan is an Air Force reservist, recreation employee, as well as a full time student at Old Dominion University. She grew up in Virginia Beach, VA. Mercedes graduated from Green Run High school in 2013, where she participated in basketball, track, theatre, and ROTC. When she is not in class she is constantly engaging her niece and nephew in arts and crafts. She plans on becoming a community counselor in her father's hometown of Baltimore. Go Ravens!

CPSIA information can be obtained
at www.ICGtesting.com
Printed in the USA
BVOW05s2053270517
485118BV00016B/61/P

9 781489 708069